BATTLE
TO THE END

BASED ON THE *STAR WARS REBELS* EPISODES
"CALL TO ACTION" BY GREG WEISMAN & SIMON KINBERG,
"REBEL RESOLVE" BY CHARLES MURRAY & HENRY GILROY, AND
"FIRE ACROSS THE GALAXY" BY SIMON KINBERG

WRITTEN BY MICHAEL KOGGE

PRESS

Los Angeles • New York

Visit the official *Star Wars* website: www.starwars.com

PROLOGUE

Like the thunderhead

of an approaching storm, the Imperial Star
Destroyer *Sovereign* bellowed through the
skies above Lothal Capital City. Yet the
massive warship neither rained turbolaser fire
nor unleashed the lightning of its ion cannons,
as it had done many times before. Instead, a
single shuttle launched from its hangar bay.
TIE fighters left their flight patterns around
the destroyer to escort the shuttle toward the
city's domed Imperial complex.

In the complex's hangar, Agent Kallus
questioned whether he would have preferred a

downpour of lasers. The sudden arrival of the shuttle—and the man inside it—did not bode well.

The most elite Imperial soldiers and officers on Lothal had been assembled as a welcome party. As the TIEs veered off and the shuttle landed, AT-DP walker pilots and stormtroopers stood at attention in long rows. Kallus couldn't locate Academy Commandant Aresko or Taskmaster Grint among the ranks, but the Inquisitor was there, his pale face impossible to read. Minister Tua, who was currently leading Lothal's government, was also present. Kallus noticed a quiver in her usually perfect posture when a thin man in a gray uniform exited the shuttle.

"Grand Moff Tarkin. I am honored by your visit to Lothal," Tua said, the quiver also detectable in her speech.

Tarkin strode up to her with a squad of black-pauldroned troopers. His aristocratic nose had the sharp contours of a hawkbat's beak, and his eyes lay sunken into his skull, which rimmed them in perpetual shadow. Though his voice sounded gracious, his words were not. "My visit is hardly an honor, Minister."

"I admit I was surprised to learn you were coming." Tua fell in step alongside Tarkin as he walked toward the complex. Kallus followed with the Inquisitor.

"I, too, have been surprised by what's been happening on your little backwater world," Tarkin said.

Tua let out a nervous chuckle. "If you are referring to the insurgents, I—"

Tarkin halted and faced her. "You have had a single, simple objective, Minister: to protect the Empire's industrial interests here, interests that are vital to our expansion throughout the Outer Rim. But instead of protecting those interests, you have allowed a cell of insurgents to flourish right under your nose. Am I correct?"

Tua cleared her throat, having nothing to say.

"And, Agent Kallus," Tarkin said, turning around, "have you just stood idly by while this rabble have attacked our men, destroyed our property, and disrupted our trade?"

Kallus was ashamed to have to report his failure. "I have exhausted every resource to capture them, sir. This group has proven quite elusive."

"It's said their leader is a Jedi," Tua added.

"Yes, let us not forget the sudden appearance of a Jedi, as if leaping from the pages of ancient history," Tarkin said in mock amusement. He shifted his glare to the Inquisitor. "A shame we don't have *someone* who specializes in dealing with them. Otherwise, our problem might be solved."

The Inquisitor bristled at Tarkin's comment in a rare display of emotion.

"Minister, have you ever met a Jedi?" Tarkin asked.

"No, I—"

"I actually knew the Jedi," Tarkin said. "Not from the pages of folklore or children's tales but as flesh and blood. And do you know what happened to them?"

"Well," Tua said, "there were rumors that—"

"They *died*," Tarkin said, interrupting her. "Every last one of them." He swept his withering gaze across all. "So you see, this criminal cannot be what he claims to be, and I shall prove it."

Kallus reconsidered his previous doubts. Perhaps the Grand Moff's arrival was for the better. Perhaps Tarkin could provide the resources Kallus needed to catch these vile insurgents—these *rebels*.

PART 1
CALL TO
ACTION

CHAPTER 1

Like most fifteen-year-olds, Ezra was a rebel. But unlike his peers, he was the real deal. Because he wasn't just breaking a curfew set by his parents or playing pranks on his teachers; he was rebelling against a tyrannical empire that had taken his parents from him and forced him onto the streets.

Most of the time, being that kind of rebel was terrifying, because one false move meant he could lose his life—or worse, his friends could lose theirs. But once in a while, it was fun. Like now.

Ezra zipped across Lothal's golden-green plains on a speeder bike filled with supplies stolen from Taskmaster Grint's weekly convoy. His friends Kanan and Sabine raced with him on speeder bikes packed with more supplies. Five Imperial troopers pursued on military-grade bikes while a troop transport in the charge of Commandant Aresko and Taskmaster Grint chugged to keep up.

Out front, Kanan course corrected toward the town of Jalath, so as to lead the Imperials far away from the *Ghost*, the freighter Ezra now called home base.

Townspeople scattered and street vendors lobbed curses as the rebels and troopers tore through the main drag. Sabine pulled back on her throttle and swerved, a move her nearest pursuer couldn't duplicate. The trooper's bike wiped out on the pavement.

Another trooper started blasting away at Kanan and Ezra. As if he was part of a speeder show, Kanan spun around in his seat, drew his blaster, and, with a single shot, took the offending trooper off his bike.

Sabine regrouped with them in a plaza; then they veered down an alley. Two of the three remaining troopers followed them into the alley while, Ezra assumed, the third was looping around to cut the rebels off.

The troopers obviously didn't know whom they were dealing with. Ezra slammed the brakes of his speeder and made a hand signal to Kanan and Sabine. They halted their speeder bikes and quickly knocked out the two troopers. When the third trooper arrived at the other end of the alley, two riderless bikes glided past him into the street.

The trooper dismounted and walked down the alley, blaster in hand. Clinging to a balcony in the alley wall above, Ezra waited until the trooper had discovered the unmoving bodies of his comrades before he made his presence known with a snort.

The trooper looked up only to have Ezra deliver a stun bolt from the blaster extension he'd attached to his lightsaber hilt. The trooper

joined his comrades in unconsciousness.

"Told ya that'd work," Ezra said. He dropped down from the balcony, as did Kanan and Sabine.

"Such a Zeb maneuver," Sabine said, her multicolored Mandalorian helmet filtering her voice. "He'd be so proud."

As they got onto their vehicles, Ezra beamed with pride, though not because of anything Zeb might've said or thought. What mattered was that Sabine was the one who had given him the compliment.

After a long stretch of traveling, they came to a circle of ancient standing stones that had become a favorite hiding spot for the *Ghost*. They parked their speeders and went aboard. Instead of receiving a welcome, however, they found their three crewmates—burly Zeb, the crotchety astromech droid Chopper, and even their ever-resourceful Twi'lek pilot, Hera— in the freighter's main cabin, all eyes and photoreceptors glued to a Holonet broadcast.

Alton Kastle, the Imperial Holonews anchor, was interviewing the former renegade Gall Trayvis, who had betrayed the rebels' cause.

"Senator Trayvis, now that you've recommitted yourself to the Empire, will your followers do the same?"

Trayvis smiled for the holocam. "Most will, Alton. These were good people who simply wanted to make the Empire a better place—peacefully. But I'm afraid these 'insurgents' have twisted my message into something violent and frightening."

The broadcast cut to grainy holograms of the *Ghost*'s ragtag bunch. Ezra flinched at seeing himself. Did he really look like that? He'd always wanted to be on the news—but not like this. Most of what was being said about him and his friends was bald-faced lies.

Trayvis spoke over the holograms. "So I'm personally offering a reward for their capture—"

"*Karabast.*" Zeb cursed in his native Lasat tongue. "Shut it off."

Hera keyed a console, and the holograms vanished. "Still makes me sick to think that Trayvis is working for the Empire."

"Well, I have a plan that might just even the score," Kanan said. "Because if Trayvis can do it, we can do it, too."

"What, we're gonna send out some kind of inspirational message?" grunted Zeb. He'd become more sarcastic since he'd been rooming with Ezra.

"Exactly," Kanan said.

Ezra braced himself before listening to the Jedi's plan. If Kanan had an idea, it probably meant they were about to do something crazy and jump into a sarlacc pit of danger.

CHAPTER 2

As was his custom, Agent Kallus arrived ten standard minutes early for the meeting Grand Moff Tarkin had called. Minister Tua and the Inquisitor came a few minutes later. Tarkin sat at his desk in the office he had occupied at the complex. He did not say a word, so neither did they. They stood and waited. Two chairs before the desk remained empty.

The first rays of dawn fell through the window, casting the city outside in crimson. It was Kallus's favorite time of day. The sun wasn't bright, and all was quiet, under control—secure.

The door hissed open. "Commandant Cumberlayne Aresko and Taskmaster Myles Grint reporting," said Aresko, the leader of Lothal's Imperial Academy. He and Grint, whose bulky frame didn't line up with Imperial fitness regulations, saluted in the doorway.

Tarkin wasted no time with military protocol. "Gentlemen, sit."

Aresko and Grint did as ordered, though Kallus could see they were nervous, especially when the Inquisitor prowled across the room toward them.

"I understand you have experience dealing with these insurgents," Tarkin said.

"Yessir," Aresko said.

"We responded personally to an attack last night in one of the outlying towns," Grint piped up, sounding enthusiastic about what Kallus had learned from the morning intelligence bulletin had been a failure. Tarkin would probably know that, too.

Aresko admitted defeat before he could be

caught. "The insurgents stole some supplies and escaped on speeder bikes," Aresko said, "but no casualties."

"No casualties," Tarkin repeated. "Your rebel cell is more principled than others."

"There are other cells?" Grint asked.

"Cells, factions, tribes, call them what you will. They lack the one thing that would make them a credible threat to the Empire," Tarkin said. "Unity."

The Inquisitor's shadow fell over the officers. Both men shifted uncomfortably in their seats. Tarkin rose from his desk. "While your cell seems uninterested in violence, it does present a specific threat—the 'Jedi.'"

"Uh, we have encountered him, sir, and he lives up to their reputation," Aresko said.

The Grand Moff walked around the desk toward the commandant and the taskmaster. "I am not concerned with his skills as a warrior. I am concerned with what he represents. Or perhaps I should say I am concerned by what you *allow* him to represent by failing to stop him." He sneered when he spit out the next word: "Hope."

Kallus observed the Inquisitor's hand hovering over his belt as Tarkin stopped before the officers. "And that, gentlemen, is something I cannot have."

The Inquisitor ignited his lightsaber. In a blur of red, Aresko and Grint went silent and still in their chairs, never to move again.

Minister Tua covered her mouth and gasped. Kallus, normally immune to such grisly sights, flinched. Aresko and Grint, though incompetent, had been loyal Imperials—a fact that didn't seem to matter at all to Grand Moff Tarkin.

"Make no mistake." The Grand Moff glanced at both Tua and Kallus. "From now on, failure will have consequences."

Tarkin gave Kallus a new directive to dispatch probe droids across Lothal to locate the rebels. Kallus then left the office and went

out into the dawn. The streets were quiet, with most citizens asleep in their beds. Everything was under control except his own mind. He kept replaying the scene in the office, with a minor alteration.

He sat in one of those chairs.

• • •

In the *Ghost*'s main cabin, Ezra fiddled with the holotransmitter he had taken from his parents' old home. He sensed something wasn't quite right with the device, yet when both he and Hera had double-checked the components, everything seemed to be in working order. He just didn't want to be responsible for botching the mission.

Kanan's plan called for them to take control of the Empire's main communications tower on Lothal. Ezra had helped scope out the tower's defenses, which included a stormtrooper perimeter guard and three antiaircraft guns at the tower's base. Kanan figured Sabine and Zeb could drive their speeders past the stormtroopers and take control of the antiaircraft guns. While Hera manned the *Phantom*, Kanan and Ezra would arrive with Chopper, and they would enter the tower. Chopper would then upload a data spike Sabine had designed into the tower's central computer. The spike would create a temporary overload of the tower's systems and allow Kanan to connect the holotransmitter to the tower and send his message of resistance to the entire galaxy.

As complicated as it was, the plan seemed nowhere near as difficult as other missions they'd done before. They should pull this one off with flying colors. Yet for some reason, Ezra had a bad feeling about it.

Kanan sensed his reluctance and asked Ezra to go outside for a walk. Ezra went but stopped on the *Ghost*'s landing ramp. He stared at the horizon, at the never-ending sea of gold-green grass.

"I'm not sure we should go through with this. My parents spoke out, and I lost them. And I don't"—Ezra tried not to choke on the words—"I don't want to lose you guys, okay? Not over this."

Kanan did not reply with a quote from some long-dead Jedi, as he often did these days. Rather, his next words had a reassuring,

almost gentle tone. "All of us have lost things. And we will take more losses before this is over. But we can't let that stop us from taking risks. We have to move forward. And when the time comes, we have to be ready to sacrifice for something bigger."

"That sounds good," Ezra said. "But it's not easy."

"It's not easy for me, either," Kanan said. "My master tried to show me, but I don't think I ever understood it until now, trying to teach it to you. I guess you and I are learning these things together."

They both looked out at the horizon. Never-ending though it seemed, Ezra knew that somewhere out there, near or far, the grass stopped growing.

Kallus received footage from a probe droid he'd dispatched near the communications tower. A wild animal had somehow busted its repulsor unit, but its mechanical eye

remained operational. It had recorded three figures racing away from the tower on speeder bikes. He couldn't see the figures clearly enough to identify them, but the speeder bikes matched the ones responsible for the theft near Jalath. The rebels must have been doing reconnaissance on the tower.

He showed the footage to Tarkin in his office, also finding the Inquisitor there, like a Loth-bat in the eaves.

"We can't risk losing the tower," Kallus advised. "We should reinforce security—"

"No," Tarkin said. "Let them believe they still possess the element of surprise. Lure them in, and we shall be waiting."

That did not seem like a sound strategy to Kallus, considering how these rebels had been able to break into a heavily guarded detainment facility on Stygeon. Nonetheless, he was not one to question a Grand Moff. "As you wish," Kallus said, exiting the room.

He slowed his steps just enough to hear Tarkin's words to the Inquisitor: "I am giving you the opportunity to redeem yourself. Remember, I want this 'Jedi' alive."

Kallus comforted himself with the fact that even the Inquisitor had to answer to Grand Moff Tarkin.

CHAPTER **3**

The Empire's main

communications tower stood out on the plains like a dark finger pointing to the heavens, blocking a vast patch of the starry sky from view. The enormous structure dwarfed all the other towers on Lothal, for good reason. The Empire had built the tower to route communications not only across Lothal but also to neighboring star systems.

Kanan and Ezra watched from a safe distance as Sabine executed her stage of the plan. On a speeder bike carrying a barrel of rhydonium fuel, she accelerated through the stormtrooper perimeter. Caught off guard, the

FREEDOM FIGHTER
SABINE

stormtroopers fired wildly and missed. The
gunners at the antiaircraft batteries had more
warning, but their bulky weapons were meant
to target larger vessels, not speeder bikes.
Before they could get a lock on her, Sabine
soared past their firing radius and steered
straight toward a gun turret. Slamming
the bike's foot pedals into the lock position,

she dove off the speeder while it continued to fly at the turret. What resulted was no mere crash but a spectacular *ka-boom* that knocked troopers off their feet and completely destroyed the turret.

Sabine jumped up to get a better view. Kanan guessed she was smiling under her helmet. Rhydonium was her favorite fuel for a reason: it was highly explosive.

The troopers and the two other turrets all turned to attack Sabine. No one noticed Zeb zooming in behind them. He hopped off his bike, landed on a turret, and hurled the gunner out of his seat. Taking control of the trigger, he blasted the other antiaircraft gun to pieces.

Kanan and Ezra then rode in, with Chopper on the back of Ezra's bike. Zeb provided cover with his cannon as they all hustled through the tower doors, which were unlocked. Startled by the sudden alarms that blared, low-level Imperials bustled about until Sabine stunned them with precision shots. Kanan yanked off a control panel and shut off the alarms.

Chopper extracted Sabine's data spike from his dome and rolled to a console. He inserted the spike into an outlet and began the upload.

Everything was going according to plan.

Then Ezra looked out the doors. "Time's up," he said.

Kanan went to Ezra's side at the door. Three Imperial gunships descended from the air, and two troop transports approached from the freeway. Though Zeb's cannon eliminated one gunship, he knew there was no way they would be able to repel the rest. Particularly when he felt a dark presence among the Imperials.

The Inquisitor was leading the attack.

"Sabine, we got targets incoming. Let's move." Kanan told Ezra to grab Zeb, then commed Hera to change the pickup point from the front of the tower to its top. She wasn't happy, but there was no other way they could evade the troopers that were in the transports.

Sabine and Chopper finished the upload and removed the data spike just as Ezra returned with Zeb. Kanan ordered them all back into the tower's turbolift.

"What about you?" Ezra asked.

Kanan ignited his lightsaber. "I'll take the next one."

Blaster bolts sizzled through the air around them. "Let's go," Zeb said, gesturing for Ezra to come inside the tower. The boy stepped back, but Kanan could sense his worry in the Force.

"Ezra, I'll be right behind you," he said. They looked at each other for a moment; then Zeb closed the tower doors.

Kanan blocked the entrance and waited for the Imperials. The transports halted just outside the doors. Stormtroopers funneled out from hatches, Agent Kallus with them. "Now this is a familiar situation," Kallus said, spotting Kanan.

"Same situation, same ending," Kanan said. "You lose."

INQUISITOR

"I don't think so," Kallus said.

One of the gunships circled the tower's summit while the other descended to the entrance. The second ship's hatch opened, and out leapt the Inquisitor.

Kanan swung his blade and slashed the portal control panel, shutting the tower doors for good. Given the Imperials' firepower, such an action wouldn't delay them for long. But every second was precious in helping his crewmates escape. And before the Imperials made it to the doors, they would have to deal with him.

The Inquisitor was the first to come forward, his red blade hissing. "What did you hope to gain by coming here?"

"You're clever. Figure it out," Kanan said, and attacked.

Their blades met, locked, disengaged, then locked again. Energy crackled as each tried to push the other back. Finally, both withdrew.

"You've been practicing," the Inquisitor said.

"Nice of you to notice," Kanan replied.

The Inquisitor grinned. "There's someone who wants to meet you. If you surrender now, he might let your friends live."

Kanan stood straight and seemed to consider the Inquisitor's proposition. He retracted his blade, as if in surrender.

"Unexpected," the Inquisitor said, still on guard.

"We're full of surprises," Kanan said.

His comm beeped and lasers suddenly lit up the sky. The Inquisitor, Kallus, and the stormtroopers looked up to see the Inquisitor's gunship explode from unexpected fire. The small auxiliary craft the rebels had dubbed the *Phantom* streaked through its debris.

Kanan had retracted his blade to signal Hera to strike. Now he used the confusion of the moment to reignite his lightsaber and attack.

It was not enough; the Inquisitor blocked

all Kanan's thrusts. Nor did the explosion of the remaining gunship—which Kanan assumed to be the handiwork of Sabine and her detonators—surprise the Inquisitor again. It further incensed him, and he struck back at Kanan with great fury. Soon Kanan lost his advantage and was pushed back toward the base of the tower.

Ezra's voice echoed over the tumult of combat. "Kanan!"

Kanan glanced up to see the *Phantom* hovering at the top of the tower, its rear hatch opening. Sabine, Zeb, and Chopper sprang inside. But Ezra hesitated, staring down at Kanan, until laser fire from the troop transports forced him to go through the hatch.

The Inquisitor lunged with ferocious speed. Kanan managed to duck and grabbed his comm. "Spectre-Two, get out of here!"

As he continued to dodge and block, Hera's voice crackled over his comm: "Not an option, Kanan!"

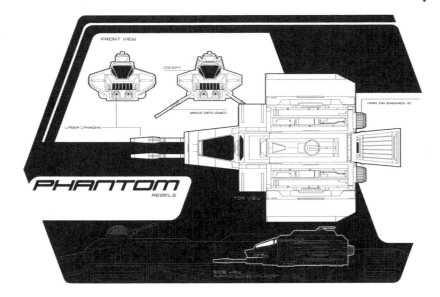

FRONT VIEW

COCKPIT

WINGS DEPLOYED

LASER CANNONS

MAIN ION ENGINES (2)

PHANTOM
REBELS

TOP VIEW

SIDE VIEW
PHANTOM DOCKED WITH GHOST

"No time—go!" he shouted, leaping away from a would-be finishing blow.

The *Phantom* rocked in the sky, taking hit after hit from the troop transports' cannons. Kanan couldn't fight the Inquisitor and try to persuade his crewmates to leave at the same time. Pinned against the tower, deflecting the Inquisitor's strokes, he yelled his best friend's name—"Hera!"—adding urgency through the Force.

Though the *Phantom* swayed in the air for a moment, Hera did as he requested. The hatch closed, and the craft turned away from the tower, braving enemy fire to shoot off into the night.

The Inquisitor also saw the ship's departure and relented in his attack, though Kanan could not have blocked if he had tried. He had no energy left. He fell to his knees.

The Inquisitor pointed the tip of his blade at Kanan's throat. But Kanan realized it was an empty threat. The Inquisitor would have killed him earlier otherwise. "Looks like I have time to meet your friend after all," Kanan said.

Agent Kallus, watching all this from the background, made a comm call. The stormtroopers put Kanan in shackles. Kanan did not resist.

CHAPTER 4

At sunrise, another Imperial
gunship landed. A man as slender as a knife
disembarked and walked toward them. Kanan
recognized him immediately, even though
the man was helmeted: Grand Moff Tarkin,
governor of the Outer Rim Territories.

Tarkin walked over to them, a thin smile on
his thin lips. "Well done, Inquisitor. These are
the results I expected." He turned to Kanan.
"So . . . you are the 'Jedi' in question?"

"Whatever you want from me, you won't get
it," Kanan said.

"Sir, we have a problem," Kallus said,
hurrying to Tarkin's side. "It appears the

insurgents have gained control of the tower's transmitter."

Kallus held up his comlink, which was broadcasting Ezra's voice. He didn't sound at all like the sarcastic boy Kanan taught, but strong and clear like the man of fierce conviction Kanan knew he was becoming.

"We have been called criminals, but we are not. We are *rebels*, fighting for the people, fighting for *you*." Kanan smiled while Tarkin scowled. Ezra's broadcast continued. "See what the Empire has done to your lives, your families, and your freedom—"

Tarkin motioned to the gunship captain. "Have all gunships in the vicinity launch their rockets at the tower."

The captain nodded and relayed the orders.

"Governor," Kallus countered, "you know a strike of that magnitude will destroy the communications tower?"

"Precisely," Tarkin said. He boarded his gunship, and Kallus and the Inquisitor followed, with Kanan held prisoner between them.

When the rockets began to hit the tower, Tarkin turned to Kanan. "You do not know what it takes to win a war. But I do."

Kanan glared at Tarkin. The Inquisitor might emanate the dark side, but the Grand Moff was a man of colder, purer evil.

Tarkin had to be stopped, at all costs, or the galaxy would suffer greatly.

For years, Ezra had mimicked voices he'd heard, particularly Imperial ones, in mocking defiance. Never in a heartbeat did he think that ability would come to good use. But when addressing the holotransmitter in the main cabin of the *Ghost*, he relied on it to speak with confidence, despite feeling otherwise.

"It's only going to get worse, unless we stand up and fight back. And it won't be easy. There'll be loss," he said, taking a breath to remember Kanan, "and there will be sacrifice.

But we can't back down just because we're
afraid. That's when we need to stand the
tallest."

Hera strode out of the shadows to join Ezra
before the camera. Chopper wheeled in next;
then Zeb plodded over. Sabine was the last, yet
stood right by Ezra's side.

"Stand up together. Because that's when we're strongest," Ezra told his invisible audience, "as one."

Static suddenly burst through the comm unit, and the holotransmitter's camera shuttered. The Imperials must have found a way to cut off their connection to the tower.

"Was it worth it?" Ezra asked. "You think anybody heard?"

"I have a feeling they did," Hera said.

Ezra exhaled and looked at his crewmates—his family. They seemed so much smaller without Kanan. "This isn't over," he said.

The Empire might have taken his parents, but they would not take his Jedi Master.

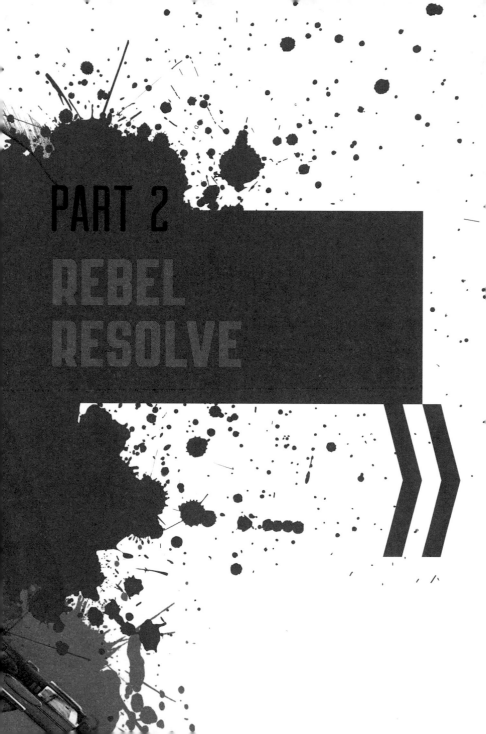

PART 2

REBEL
RESOLVE

CHAPTER 5

After docking the *Phantom* with its mother ship, the *Ghost*, Hera went into her personal cabin. She had received an encrypted call over the holonet from a very important contact. Hera accepted the message, and Fulcrum's distorted voice, scrambled beyond recognition, filled her cabin. "Kanan knew the risks and had accepted them. I'm sorry, but you must focus on your next objective."

Hera was insulted that Fulcrum would give up on Kanan so easily. "Kanan *is* our objective. We can still find him."

"At what cost? You? Your unit? The overall mission?" Fulcrum asked. "There's something

REBEL PILOT
HERA

else, Hera. The transmission Ezra was able to beam out has attracted attention, and not just from civilians but from the highest levels of the Empire."

Hera hesitated. Perhaps her contact had a point. Fulcrum was always considering the long-term strategy. "It was Kanan's plan. I guess it worked," she said.

"Your mission was to be unseen,

unnoticed," Fulcrum lectured. "And now—"

Hera spoke out in defense of her friend. "Kanan wanted to inspire people. He wanted to give them hope."

"Well, he was successful," Fulcrum said. "But if you are caught—if Ezra is caught—that hope will die. To protect your unit, and Ezra, you must stop your search for Kanan and go into hiding. Do you understand?"

Fulcrum's last words were not a question but a command. The transmission ended, and she sat on her bunk. Where did her loyalties lie? With her best friend or with the growing rebellion?

She knew what Kanan would tell her: "Forget about me. Stay focused on the mission. Do as Fulcrum requests."

It was the same thing she would have told Kanan if she had been the one captured. Part of her wished she had been so she wouldn't have to make this kind of decision.

• • •

Ezra gathered Sabine and Zeb in the *Ghost*'s common room, where they studied a map of Lothal to try to determine where Kanan was being held. It was frustrating, because that place could be anywhere on the planet.

"Odds are they've still got him at the Imperial complex," Sabine said.

"If they do, we all know he's as good as gone," Zeb said.

Ezra fumed at such talk. "He's not gone! And he's not in the Imperial complex!"

"How do you know that?" Zeb asked.

"I just know!" He stalked around the room, wishing he could explain how. But that would be impossible, because he couldn't explain it to himself. All the Force told him was that his master was somewhere out there, still alive.

Sabine wouldn't be convinced. "We can't make a plan based on a feeling."

"Yes, we can—we do it all the time!" Ezra said. Didn't they remember the mission to Stygeon Prime or to the asteroid where the fyrnocks lurked? All their plans had been based on Kanan's feelings.

"Not this time," Hera said as she entered the common room, looking exhausted and somber, as if she had just attended a funeral. "We can't risk it."

"Can't? Or won't?" Ezra couldn't believe what he was hearing. These were Kanan's friends—his *family*.

"Ezra," Hera said gently, "there's a bigger mission you're not seeing. We can't be jeopardized for one soldier."

"Soldier? He's our friend. He'd do whatever it took to protect us."

"He already did when he sacrificed himself for us," Hera said. "He'd want us to honor the choice he made."

Sabine and Zeb seemed to accept Hera's command without argument. Ezra stormed out, wanting to yell at all of them. But he couldn't get out the words. Because deep down, he knew Hera was right.

CHOPPER

The problem was he also knew *he* was right.

He went into the cabin he shared with Zeb to do what he had never done on his own before. He meditated, like his master. Maybe the Force would inspire him. Maybe it would devise a plan to save Kanan.

When he opened his eyes, he found himself standing in the doorway of Kanan's cabin. He didn't remember walking there. But he accepted it, like he accepted that Chopper was also in the cabin, looking around and beeping softly, as if mourning Kanan's loss like a living being.

"I miss him, too," Ezra said. "But I have a plan to find him. Wanna help?"

The droid, one of the great naysayers of the universe, chirped an emphatic yes. Now all Ezra had to do was persuade Sabine and Zeb to do likewise.

CHAPTER 6

"I will ask you again.

Where is your rebel hideout?"

When Kallus received no response from Kanan Jarrus, he ordered the interrogation droid to administer another dose of truth serum. The droid floated forward and poked the rebel prisoner with one of the many needles that stuck out of its ball-shaped body. After the droid withdrew the needle and floated back, Kanan twitched in his restraining chair.

"It's only a matter of time before he breaks," Kallus told Tarkin, who had come to watch the most recent session.

Tarkin snorted. "You have wasted enough of my time."

The door opened and the Inquisitor entered the detention cell. He strode forward, casting a dismissive glance at the droid and Kallus. "You are no doubt unaware that Jedi are trained to resist mind probes."

Kallus frowned. Not only was he following standard Imperial interrogation procedure, but no one in his experience had ever been able to resist the truth serum. It just took time.

Tarkin, however, seemed intrigued. "If he is the Jedi he claims to be, I take it you have a solution?"

"Pain," the Inquisitor said as if it was obvious. "The Jedi still feels pain. And pain can break anyone."

He stretched out his black-gloved hand. Kanan's head suddenly shot forward, stopping centimeters from the Inquisitor's palm. "You will tell me where to find your rebel friends," the Inquisitor said.

Kanan seemed to bob in and out of consciousness, his speech slurred. "No . . . Ezra . . . not him."

The Inquisitor leaned closer. "What do you see?"

"I see . . ." Kanan's eyes rolled back, and he shook off his grogginess with a smile. "I see you, growing more and more frustrated."

The Inquisitor was not pleased. "How perceptive. Perhaps you can help alleviate my frustration."

The Inquisitor gestured with a finger, activating a feature of the chair Kallus had reserved for the final stage of interrogation. Kanan's binders sparked, conducting electricity through his body.

Kallus left the detention cell, realizing his presence was no longer required. He could hear Kanan's cries far down the hallway.

None revealed the location of the rebel hideout.

CHAPTER 7

Sabine landed the *Phantom* outside the ancient stone circle, near another starship, the *Broken Horn*. Ezra gave her a reassuring nod as they joined Zeb leaving the ship. Ezra's pleas to save Kanan had won over Sabine, and once she agreed to ignore Hera's orders, Zeb followed suit. Still, Ezra felt guilty about defying Hera. She had done so much for him, and now he was repaying her with disobedience. She deserved better.

He walked over to the gangster they'd dealt with on many occasions, Cikatro Vizago. The green-skinned Devaronian, whose split left horn matched the name of his vessel, was overseeing his enforcer droids as they carried cargo crates into his freighter. He raised an eye ridge when he saw Ezra. "This is unexpected. Looking for work, or something else?"

Sabine and Zeb stood behind Ezra as he spoke. "My guess is you already know why we're here."

Vizago hesitated, as if thinking over his words. "I don't know where your friend is. I'm sorry."

It was a lame apology. Ezra took a step closer. "You must've heard something?"

"Even if I did know something, it would be of no use to you. In fact, I think your activities got the Empire's attention and have made things more difficult for me. So get out of here. You're bad luck." Vizago went to board his own ship.

In the past, Ezra would have overreacted. But because of what Kanan had taught him, he let go of his anger. "Ever wonder why the Empire was so interested in Kanan? Why

56

they'd send an Inquisitor to Lothal?"

Sabine removed her helmet. "Ezra, don't."

Vizago turned around. "No. Please, do."

All eyes suddenly fell on Ezra, even the photoreceptors of Vizago's enforcers. Ezra hadn't planned what to say next, so he just told the truth: "Because Kanan is a Jedi."

Vizago laughed. "Kanan? A Jedi? You're funny, kid. That scoundrel couldn't be a Jedi any more than you could."

Ezra recalled how much Kanan despised dealing with the gangster. Now Ezra felt the same way. But he needed the information Vizago had. So he closed his eyes, extended his hand, and, sinking himself into the Force, imagined the stack of Vizago's crates. He pictured one crate levitating from the stack and moving in Vizago's direction.

Vizago stopped laughing. When Ezra opened his eyes, Vizago was staring up in shock at a crate that hovered over him. He dove for cover.

Ezra let the crate fall. It thudded in the dirt.

"You," Vizago said, picking himself up, "*you* are a Jedi?"

"And so is Kanan." Ezra steeled his voice, aware that Kanan would despise what he was about to offer. "Help me and you'll have a Jedi owing you a favor."

Vizago showed a needle-toothed grin. "Come with me, boy. Alone."

Neither Zeb nor Sabine said anything, but their glances told Ezra to be wary. Vizago could be trusted only as long as the situation benefited him.

Ezra followed the gangster into the *Broken Horn,* behind droids restacking crates in the cargo hold. "Look," Vizago said, "ever since you blew up the Empire's comm tower—"

"That wasn't us," Ezra said.

"—they have no long-range communications," Vizago continued. "So they've started using these." Vizago took out a datapad, pressed a button, and projected the image of what looked like an astromech droid, although with Imperial markings.

"Droid couriers," Vizago said. "They take data from the city up to their communication ship in orbit."

"What kind of data?" Ezra asked.

"Everything. You name it—personnel, weapons, deployments"—Vizago paused, as if for dramatic effect—"prisoners."

"Kanan?"

"Possibly, but I can't guarantee that," Vizago said.

Ezra shook his head. Vizago never could guarantee any of his information. It was a shame they couldn't deal with someone else. "So what do you need in return?"

Vizago chewed it over with a smile. "Today, nothing. Tomorrow, who knows? I'll call you when I want to collect."

Ezra didn't like that part of the bargain, but he didn't have a choice. He exited the *Broken Horn* and walked up to Sabine and Zeb. Their backs were to him as they conversed with someone—maybe one of Vizago's droids?

"It's okay, guys. I have a lead—"

Sabine and Zeb turned around, revealing that the third member of their conversation wasn't a droid, but Hera! "For what you just bargained, you better have something more than a lead!" she said, heading back to the *Ghost*.

Ezra rushed after her. "Hera, I know you're mad, but—"

"Mad? Try furious. You just put all our lives in jeopardy. I gave you a direct order and you disobeyed me."

Ezra understood how she felt. But she'd taught him that being a rebel meant sometimes you didn't play by the rules. "It paid off. I know how to find where Kanan is," he stated, before adding with less certainty, "maybe."

Hera stopped at the *Ghost*'s landing ramp but kept her back to Ezra. "Maybe? All that for 'maybe'?"

"Hera, none of us want to give up on Kanan," Ezra said as Sabine and Zeb joined him.

The tips of Hera's head-tails curled, a Twi'lek sign of aggravation. "And you think I do?"

"No, I don't," Ezra said. "That's why I took this risk."

Hera sighed, then faced them. "What did you learn?"

"I have a plan," Ezra said, looking up the landing ramp, where an orange-and-white astromech droid waited in the hatch. "And it involves Chopper."

CHAPTER 8

Chopper buzzed nervously while Sabine gave him a new paint job. Each spray of black and white paint made him look more and more like an Imperial courier droid and less and less like himself.

"It's for Kanan," Ezra said. "We'll paint you back fresh and new once we rescue him."

They'd better paint him back. Chopper detested being mistaken for a model with an inferior central processor. But he didn't grumble as much as he normally would. His probability module determined that his temporary paint job would indeed increase their chances of finding Kanan.

At the Capital City spaceport, Sabine and Zeb took out a squad of stormtroopers and stole the accompanying courier droid. It was Chopper's job to replace the droid.

"I know you can do this, Chopper," Ezra said to him.

It was almost an insult: Chopper could play this role with 93 percent of his circuits off-line. Imperials didn't program their droids with personalities. All they wanted were beeps of yes and no.

Chopper wheeled into the hangar where the stormtroopers had been leading the courier droid. Two troopers guarded the ramp of a transport shuttle.

"There's the courier, but where's his escort?" one trooper said to the other.

"Not our problem. We're running late as it is," his comrade said. He waited for Chopper to roll up the ramp before he spoke into his wrist comm. "BN-Seven Forty-Nine to pilot. Courier is aboard."

Chopper planted his treads on the cabin floor as the shuttle took off. The cockpit blast doors were open, so once the shuttle had gained orbit, his photoreceptor made out their destination in the viewscreen. They were heading toward a light cruiser.

Chopper couldn't see the *Ghost* anywhere in the star field, which he calculated was a good thing. They were out there, flying undetected by the Imperials.

The shuttle docked with the light cruiser. Chopper went out with the troops the shuttle had ferried and switched on the beacon Sabine had installed inside him. It would allow Hera to track his location on the cruiser with the *Ghost*'s extensive passive sensors.

He trundled down the cruiser's main corridor and onto the bridge. It was a busy place. Officers conversed with the captain while technicians consulted screens and operated their various stations. "You're late, Two-Six-Four," one technician said. "Plug in."

Chopper tooted back at him in binary. He was never late. It was the shuttle pilot who was late. Chopper had one of the best internal clocks ever invented.

Following the technician's orders, he extended a connector arm from his dome and inserted it into a port. Instantly, he had access to the entire Imperial network. Given the network's size, sifting through it to find out where Kanan was being held would take three hours, forty-four minutes, and eleven seconds—too much time, according to their mission plan. So he began downloading and copying everything he could with the intent to search it all later.

The technician glanced at his monitor, which was still blank. "Where's the data? I'm not seeing it."

Chopper wanted to zap the man. Organics could be so impatient. He whistled and sent a stream of text from one of his downloaded files to the screen.

CHOPPER

"Hold it—you're not authorized to copy communication logs!"

Chopper tweedled a fake apology as he searched the files for something with the proper security clearance to display. "What's the problem here?" a nearby officer asked.

"This droid is malfunctioning, sir," said the technician.

Though he had completed downloading only 57 percent of the available data, Chopper recognized his time to complete the mission was up. He rotated the small radar dish on his dome and sent a signal to the *Ghost*. Now success depended on them.

"Looks like an older model," said the officer. "You'd better check the encryption codes."

The technician bent down to inspect Chopper. He never put a finger on the droid. An explosion suddenly shook the bridge, knocking the technician back.

"We're under attack!" yelled the officer.

Chopper disconnected just as the bridge rocked again. The console Chopper had been plugged into sparked into flame. Alarms rang out. Officers and technicians rushed about. No one paid any attention to the black-and-white courier droid heading for the turbolift.

The lift took Chopper down to the

cruiser's lower corridor. He angled straight for an emergency air lock and began to operate the controls with his manipulator. Four stormtroopers hustled past on a duty errand—only to be sucked out the air lock when Chopper opened it.

Chopper flew out with the troopers into the emptiness of space. Unlike the troopers' armored suits, he was designed to operate at full functionality in the zero-gravity environment. While the troopers tumbled and whirled, Chopper received Hera's message to "hit it" and fired his booster rocket in the direction of her transmission.

The *Ghost* peeled away from a strafing run on the cruiser to head toward Chopper. The freighter was noticeably damaged, and any of the cruiser's cannon shots might permanently cripple it. But the *Ghost* skirted the latest barrage and opened its cargo bay. Chopper burned his last bit of fuel to give his rocket maximum thrust. He shot inside the cargo

bay, and right as his booster sputtered out, his manipulator arm grabbed the ladder. He held on against the vacuum of space.

When the ship was out of the cruiser's range and descending toward Lothal, Chopper released his grip and steadied himself on the floor. Zeb, Sabine, and Ezra hurried into the bay. "That was amazing, Chopper!" Ezra said.

Chopper pumped his manipulator arm in organic fashion. Maybe in addition to a new paint job, he'd get a lubrication bath at last after all this.

After Chopper was scooped up, Ezra sat in Kanan's seat and took in the view of his home planet through the cockpit canopy. Next to him, Hera piloted the *Ghost* toward one of their hiding spots while Sabine and Chopper searched through the downloaded files. Zeb hunched in the doorway to avoid hitting his rather large head.

"I'm proud of you," Hera said to Ezra. "You stepped up and took the lead. Kanan has taught you well."

"So have you," Ezra said. It was the truth. They had *all* taught him well—even Zeb.

Sabine stopped scrolling through her datapad. "I think we found something."

Chopper projected a hologram of Kanan,

stamped with the Imperial symbol, in the air. "Kanan is on Governor Tarkin's Star Destroyer, the *Sovereign*," Sabine went on. "It's still here above Lothal, but it's scheduled to leave soon."

"Where to?" Hera asked.

"The Mustafar system," Sabine said. "I've never heard of it."

Hera's head-tails twitched, ever so slightly, and she stared out the canopy. Ezra was a novice at reading Twi'lek body language, but it was obvious she was afraid.

And Hera was *never* afraid.

"Hera?" Sabine said.

Hera let out a breath. "I've only heard the name once, from Kanan. He said Mustafar is where Jedi go to die."

Lothal's beautiful golden-green surface shone like an emerald through the canopy. Ezra did not see it. He saw only his master, bound in shackles, struggling to survive.

PART 3

FIRE ACROSS
THE GALAXY

CHAPTER 9

Imperial stormtrooper

TK-626 and his comrade MB-223 made their 109th patrol of the airfield that night. It would be an understatement to say that TK-626 was frustrated. The recruiter had told him that after a few months of joining Lothal's stormtrooper corps, he would be assigned to a Star Destroyer and be able to travel the stars. Months had passed since he had enlisted, and he was still on Lothal doing night duty with MB-223. He knew this was partially a punishment for the graffiti attack by an artist on the same airfield. Yet that was a single incident. Nothing had ever happened on their watch again. He was beginning to think he had made a mistake in joining the Empire.

"Miss me, bucket heads?" said a filtered voice behind them.

He and MB-223 spun around. A female in multicolored Mandalorian armor stood on the wall that surrounded the airfield. Though it could have been anyone under that helmet, TK-626 had no doubt she was the artist who had caused all his troubles in the first place. She carried a mini-airbrush in her hand.

There was no hesitation this time. He and MB-223 opened fire.

The artist ran along the top of the wall, leaping past their blaster bolts. "Yup, you definitely missed me."

TK-626 tongued his helmet comlink. "We have an intruder on the north side, sector nine. The *artist* is back. Sound the alarm!"

They ran after her. Alarms rang across the airfield. Stormtroopers from other patrols joined them. Together, they would ensure that there would be no graffiti that night.

Sprinting past the grounded transport ships toward the TIEs, TK-626 thought he heard voices behind him, but he didn't look. If he lost the artist, his career was finished for good. Stopping her was the only thing that might finally get him promoted out of there.

One of his shots nearly took her off the wall. "You got a little better," she said.

TK-626 concentrated his fire with MB-223. Still, somehow she dove off the wall and dodged the blasts. "But *I* got a lot better."

She climbed up the wing of a TIE fighter, then leapt to the top of the fuselage. Meanwhile, a transport lifted up from the airfield.

TK-626 checked the timetable on his helmet display. No transports were scheduled to be launched until the next day. It could only mean the transport had been hijacked by . . .

Rebels.

The artist had been a distraction for the rebels to hot-wire and steal the transport. TK-626 adjusted his aim and started shooting at the departing transport. MB-223 followed his lead. If that transport escaped, night patrol would seem like a blessing. TK-626 and his comrade would be assigned to permanent cleaning duty.

The transport's cargo lift extended downward, giving the artist a platform to leap onto. Once she got her footing, she waved down to the stormtroopers. "Bye-bye, bucket heads!"

TK-626 wanted to shoot her right then and there, but another familiar sound gave him pause. Attached to the TIE fighter the artist had climbed was a blinking, beeping red dot.

"Not again," TK-626 said. Permanent cleaning duty suddenly didn't seem so bad after all. "Everyone, evacuate!"

He and MB-223 turned and ran. When the red dot stopped beeping, TK-626 covered his head and dove to the ground.

The TIE fighter behind him exploded, setting flame to an entire row of adjacent TIEs.

After all the debris had settled, TK-626 pushed himself up. The hijacked transport whipped through the smoke of the explosion. The plumes formed the same symbol the artist had painted on a TIE wing months earlier. It had two wings swooping upward, around an avian head.

The Starbird.

TK-626 put his head back down to the ground, even though the explosion was over. The Empire had recruited him because he'd been a bully. Now he felt like a chump.

Mustafar. Like Sabine, Ezra had never heard of the planet. The *Ghost*'s navicomputer entry had little information about it, revealing only that it was a young planet with many active volcanoes.

A world where Jedi went to die, Hera had said.

Which Jedi? And why? Ezra kept asking himself these questions as he and his crewmates traveled through hyperspace toward the planet.

They had hidden the *Ghost* on Lothal and taken the stolen Imperial transport instead. In the transport, they could approach Tarkin's Star Destroyer and not be instantly blasted to ions.

But when they emerged from hyperspace, Ezra saw there was more than one Star Destroyer—there was a fleet of them, centered on the *Sovereign*. Through the cockpit canopy, they glowed like white arrowheads against the cracked volcanic surface of Mustafar. The black dots of hundreds of TIE fighters and transports winked in and out as they circled the destroyers.

"I'll send in our transponder code as soon as we know Kanan is there," Hera said, sitting in the main pilot's seat. "Ezra?"

Huddled in the cockpit, Sabine, Zeb, and Chopper all looked to Ezra. They were relying on him as never before, though he knew they were skeptical about his abilities. He was skeptical, too. Trying to sense Kanan over such a large distance was not going to be easy.

"Well, here goes nothing." Ezra closed his eyes, took a breath, and allowed the Force to flow through him. *Make a connection,* Kanan had told him. Ezra channeled himself outward, searching for a connection—the most powerful, personal connection he'd ever had with someone in his life.

As they neared the *Sovereign,* he began to feel the thousands of presences on the ship. Somewhere among them was Kanan—he hoped.

"Ezra," Hera said. "Is he there?"

CHAPTER 10

Electricity coursed from the chair into Kanan's body. He felt as if he was being fried from the inside out. Despite the torment, he gave no straight answer to the Inquisitor's questions. He only screamed.

The Inquisitor took his time walking across the detention cell before he switched off the chair's shock function. Kanan shuddered and fell forward in his binders. His body smoldered and twitched. The Inquisitor chuckled.

"Still protecting your precious crew. Quite admirable. But what I want to know is about the *other* rebels—particularly one code named Fulcrum."

Kanan repeated what he'd said during all the other sessions. "I know nothing of a larger rebellion. And if I did, I'd rather give my life than tell you."

The Inquisitor stepped closer to him. "So heroic. Just like your master."

At the mention of his master, Kanan flinched. The memory of her death hurt him more than any jolt of electricity could. The Inquisitor noticed and smiled.

"Tell me, Jedi: how did you survive Order Sixty-Six? Hmmm?"

Kanan kept his mouth shut. That was a rhetorical question meant to hurt him. He could sense that the Inquisitor already knew the answer.

"It was your master, Billaba, who laid down her life for yours," the Inquisitor said. "Do you remember her last word to you? Her last and final breath before she died?"

Kanan said nothing. The Inquisitor leaned

IMPERIAL FORCE
INQUISITOR

even closer. "You do, don't you? You see her in your sleep. You hear her voice when you wake."

The Inquisitor was speaking the truth. Master Billaba had haunted Kanan for many years after her death. Sometimes he swore he saw her phantom at the edge of his vision.

Often during meditation he still heard echoes of her voice.

"Tell me, Jedi, what was her last word to you?"

Tears wet Kanan's eyes. He remembered Master Billaba's last word as if she had said it just the day before. That one word had defined his entire existence since her death. He couldn't resist revealing it any more than he could hold back his screams.

"Run."

The Inquisitor's eyes glinted with delight. He went on with his questions. "And does your loyal and precious crew know you ran as your master fell? That you abandoned her and the Jedi Order when they needed you most? What do you think your rebels would do if they knew their leader was a coward?"

Kanan trembled. The questions needed no answer. He had been running away from them all his adult life. The Inquisitor was right. He wasn't a real rebel, just like he wasn't a real teacher. Having abandoned the Order, he wasn't even a Jedi.

He was a fake, a fraud.

The Inquisitor removed from his belt the two parts that made Kanan's lightsaber hilt. "You're even afraid of your own power. You don't have the courage to wear your full saber out in the open." He pointed the hilt at Kanan's throat. "Let me tell you something, Jedi. You're right to be afraid. You couldn't save your master then—and you can't save your followers now."

Kanan closed his eyes. He was ready for the Inquisitor to ignite the blade. Then, at least, his pain would end—and his life as a fraud would be over.

A faint yet familiar presence brushed him. His eyes shot open.

Ezra?

"He's there. He's alive," Ezra said.

Hera toggled switches on the transport's

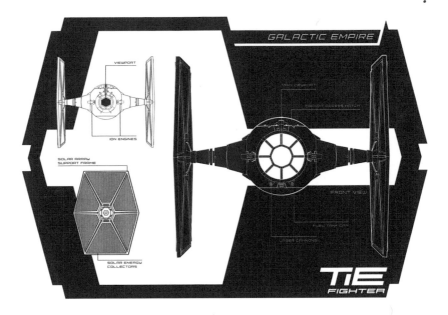

console. "Sending codes." Her voice fluttered, barely containing her emotions.

Ezra sat still. Chopper uploaded the transponder codes Fulcrum had sent weeks earlier in case of an emergency like this. The codes should mask their stolen transport's true identity.

But there was always a chance it wouldn't work. Instead of responding, the Star Destroyer might reduce them to star dust.

They might not even see the shot coming.

A voice came over the comm. "Transport ship six-three-three-seven-eight cleared for docking. We have ten TIEs inbound with reinforcements. Open bay five."

Hera cracked a smile, the first in some time. "They bought it, Chop. Send in Sabine's present."

Chopper released a TIE fighter from the transport's cargo hold and sent it toward the Star Destroyer. Ezra and Zeb had stolen the TIE while they were on a mission to get meiloorun fruits. Instead of scrapping the ship, as Kanan had ordered, they had hidden it behind a giant stone mound on Lothal. The Empire had never found it, though when Sabine learned of their secret, she couldn't help adding her painterly touch.

Ezra hoped the Imperials would admire Sabine's art long enough for the next phase of their plan to work.

CHAPTER 11

While on guard duty,

JJR-579 observed something odd about the TIE fighter the *Sovereign*'s tractor beam had just pulled inside docking bay five. He called over his fellow trooper JTN-303 and pointed out the splashes of color that were painted all over the TIE. "That's not regulation."

JTN-303 peered closer. "I kind of like it."

JJR-579 was about to question JTN-303's loyalty when his helmet comm suddenly emitted a high-pitched squeal. The sound was so piercing he couldn't hear. He couldn't even think. His head pounded in pain. He gripped his helmet, trying to get it off, but Imperial regulations made the fit tight.

As JJR-579 fell to his knees, he noticed the lights were flickering in the docking bay. Then everything went black.

Sabine wasn't just a painter. She was an artist. And good artists used all their skills when creating their best work.

In prepping the TIE fighter, she had taken inspiration from technical schematics she'd found in Chopper's downloaded files. She rigged detonators inside the cockpit to send out an electromagnetic pulse. The pulse would short-circuit all technology, from stormtrooper helmet comms to the Star Destroyer's biggest systems.

When Sabine activated the detonators, the pulse worked even better than she'd imagined. The *Sovereign* was reduced to using emergency reserves to keep life support running. Every other system was down.

With the *Sovereign*'s tractor beam and turbolasers disabled, Hera was able to dock against the side of the Star Destroyer, near the detention area. Sabine looked forward to blowing a hole into the *Sovereign*'s hull, but Ezra improvised quicker. He carved a portal with his lightsaber. They all went into the destroyer, leaving Chopper to keep the transport's engines running.

Sabine was pleased to discover the effect her art had on her audience. Stormtroopers lay unconscious on the floor of the corridor, with their hands on their helmets. But Sabine knew it was only temporary. "These guys'll wake up soon."

"How soon?" Ezra asked.

"Too soon, I reckon," Zeb said.

Ezra led them down a few corridors before Chopper radioed Hera with an urgent message. Reinforcements were on their way.

"How many troopers incoming?" Sabine asked.

"At least two transports, minimum," Hera said.

"Don't worry," Sabine said. "On a ship this big, it'll take 'em a while to find us."

Arriving at a T junction, she saw she couldn't have been more wrong. Stormtroopers rushed toward them from the corner ahead, firing their rifles. The rebels turned to run back, only to have another squad come at them from behind. These weren't your average cannon-fodder recruits. Grand Moff Tarkin commanded some of the most disciplined and experienced troops in the Empire.

Sabine fired back as Zeb, Ezra, and Hera started to do the same. But there was no way they were going to beat the odds. They headed down the only empty corridor and ran for their lives.

Farther down the corridor, a heavy blast door was closing to trap them. Quickly, each rebel leapt through the shrinking opening. As the door closed behind them, Ezra used his

FREEDOM FIGHTER EZRA

lightsaber to melt its locking controls. That would stall the troopers for a while.

Sabine was impressed. Ezra had become quite skilled with a lightsaber, considering that only a few weeks earlier he had nearly amputated his arm multiple times. "Pretty clever, kid. So what's next?"

Ezra didn't blush as he normally did when she complimented him. "Kanan is down that hall. I just cut off our only way to get to him."

"Might be *our* only way. But it's not *yours*." Hera glanced upward, at vents that circulated air. "Do what you do best, Ezra. We'll keep the troops occupied."

"You know, one day I'm going to be too big to fit in here," Ezra said.

As Ezra climbed into the vent, Sabine almost remarked that he'd always be the Loth-rat of the group. But she held her tongue, because it wasn't true anymore.

CHAPTER **12**

Kanan slumped in the chair. The Inquisitor was gone, but pain still racked his body. He was beginning to think he had imagined feeling his apprentice's presence when the door to his cell opened and Ezra stepped inside.

The boy said something Kanan couldn't process. It took all Kanan's breath to utter his next words: "You shouldn't have come here . . . but I'm glad you did."

Ezra unlocked Kanan's shackles. "You would have done the same for me. In fact, you have."

Kanan tried to stand up on his own, but his body was too weak. He fell into Ezra's arms. Though half the size of Kanan, the boy somehow found the strength to keep Kanan on his feet and lead him out.

But it was more than just the boy's being strong. Ezra was channeling his strength to Kanan. With every step he took, Kanan found his muscles a little less exhausted, his nerves beginning to calm. And that strength came from the Force. The boy was channeling it into Kanan, just as Kanan had helped Ezra heal during their mission to the asteroid base.

They faced no trouble in the detention area. All the stormtrooper guards lay on the floor, knocked out cold. Ezra explained that Sabine had built a pulse weapon from stolen Imperial files, but Kanan's head was too cloudy for him to understand. He leaned on the boy and staggered down the hall.

Ezra seemed to know where they were

going. He had memorized the layout of that section of the Star Destroyer, and said their fastest route was through the engine room. By the time they entered it, Kanan had regained enough strength to stand on his own.

He would need more than that to go any farther. There, blocking the catwalk in front of them, stood the Inquisitor.

"A chance to redeem yourself. What more can a Jedi ask for?" The Inquisitor ignited both blades of his lightsaber.

Kanan had no weapon. His lightsaber hung from the Inquisitor's belt. Yet even as weak as he was, Kanan wasn't going to let his apprentice fight the Inquisitor for him.

"Let me borrow that," Kanan said, indicating Ezra's lightsaber.

"Yeah, no problem," Ezra said.

Kanan took it and charged down the catwalk, firing Ezra's custom blaster extension. The Inquisitor easily deflected each shot, but hitting him was not Kanan's purpose. He wanted to keep his nemesis busy, away from Ezra.

When he was within striking distance, Kanan activated the blade and lunged. The Inquisitor repelled the blow, and they began to duel once again. Adrenaline surged through Kanan's muscles, pulling him away from exhaustion. He forgot about the pain in his body and focused on the fight.

It was a fight he could not—he *would not*—lose.

Their blades clashed back and forth, illuminating the haze with lines of blue and red. Every thrust was dodged; every jab was blocked. Kanan could not gain the advantage, yet neither could the Inquisitor. The two had fought so frequently that each could anticipate the other's moves.

Kanan had a new trick up his sleeve, thanks to Ezra. Between slashes, he triggered the blaster extension. The Inquisitor was

KANAN

caught by surprise and found it difficult to block both blaster bolts and Kanan's lightsaber attack. He was forced backward on the catwalk.

Then Ezra ran toward them.

Kanan wanted to tell the boy to go back—to run. But he didn't—because running was what

Kanan had done all those years. He knew it was also what Ezra had done, trying to run from the memory of losing his parents.

No. Kanan was done running. So was his Padawan learner. The two of them would fight, together. As master and apprentice.

Kanan locked his blade with the Inquisitor's. He didn't need to tell Ezra what to do next. The boy raised a hand and, with the Force, wrenched Kanan's lightsaber loose from the Inquisitor's belt. It sailed through the air into Ezra's hand.

Ezra activated the blade and leapt into the battle.

"At last, a fight that might be worthy of my time," the Inquisitor said.

Though outnumbered two to one, the Inquisitor appeared to be recharged by Ezra's attack. He struck back with a relentlessness he hadn't shown before. His parries seemed effortless, and his attacks nearly bit flesh. Ezra advanced, trying for a jab from underneath, when the Inquisitor made a sharp gesture with his hand and cast him backward with the Force. The thud of Ezra's fall rattled the catwalk floor.

The Inquisitor pivoted back to Kanan, kicking him squarely in the chest. Then he used the Force to push Kanan down the catwalk, away from Ezra. It took some effort for Kanan to get up. He was losing his adrenaline boost.

He might also be losing his apprentice. The Inquisitor sent his dual blades toward Ezra. The boy tried to deflect with his lightsaber, but the other weapon was moving too fast. It slashed Ezra across the face. In pain, Ezra dropped Kanan's lightsaber and fell from the catwalk.

Kanan stretched out with the Force. He made a tender, fatherly connection to Ezra for what might be the last time.

May the Force be with you, Ezra Bridger.

CHAPTER 13

In the darkness, Ezra heard

many voices. They all called his name: *Ezra . . .*
Ezra . . . Ezra! He heard his mother and his
father. He heard the nasal tone of his snouted
family friend, Tseebo. He also heard his new
family. Chopper's grouchy beeps. Zeb's annoyed
growls. Kanan's sober manner that could put
him to sleep. Then there was Sabine, who
made his heart skip a beat when she called him
by his real name and not "kid."

"Ezra?" Now he heard Hera's voice. "Ezra?"

He opened his eyes, and the darkness
disappeared. Hera's voice remained, loud and

clear over his comlink. "Ezra, are you out there?"

He moaned into his comlink. "I'm . . . here."

He had fallen onto a lower platform that ringed the engine. His face throbbed with a burning pain. He touched his cheek gingerly. There was no blood. The heat from the Inquisitor's lightsaber had cauterized his wound. He would be scarred forever.

"Do you have Kanan?" Hera said on the comlink. "Is he okay?"

Ezra looked up at the catwalk. There Kanan fought with an intensity Ezra had never seen. He must've picked up his old lightsaber, because he fought with both blades, one in each hand. The Inquisitor struggled to ward off the attacks and soon teetered on the edge of the catwalk.

"Yeah," Ezra radioed back. "I think he's better than okay."

His master's voice echoed through the chamber. "You were right. I was a coward. But now I know there's something stronger than fear—far stronger. The Force." Kanan brought his blade upward. "Let me show you how strong it is."

The Inquisitor held up his lightsaber and triggered his blades to spin. They whirled around the axis of his hilt like a propeller, forming a circular shield of energy.

On his downward arc, Kanan found the narrowest of gaps between the rotating blades. He sliced the Inquisitor's hilt in half.

The Inquisitor dropped the two pieces of his lightsaber. Losing his balance, he tumbled backward, saving himself from falling farther by grabbing the catwalk ledge. Below him, the engine core rumbled, shaking the room. Ezra saw that one piece of the lightsaber had lodged itself in the hyperdrive energy conduit.

The Inquisitor clung to the catwalk, fuming like the engine core. "You have no idea what you've unleashed here today. There are some things far more frightening than death."

Kanan aimed a lightsaber at the Inquisitor's throat. For a moment, Ezra thought Kanan was going to kill the Inquisitor. But his master deactivated both lightsabers and glared at the Inquisitor, saying nothing.

The Inquisitor sneered back, then released his grip on the catwalk. He plunged past Ezra and met his end somewhere below in a loud crash.

The ship rumbled. The piece of the Inquisitor's hilt was obstructing the energy flow of the hyperdrive. The engine was erupting, and there was no chance of fixing it. The *Sovereign* was going to blow.

Ezra scrambled up a ladder to the catwalk. He found his master on his knees, his head bowed toward where Ezra had fallen.

"Kanan," Ezra said.

His master turned. He looked like Ezra's parents had when, after a long day of searching, they had found Ezra wandering the spaceport alone. "I thought I lost you," he said.

Ezra smiled, even though it hurt to do so. "I know the feeling. Let's go home."

CHAPTER 14

Home was the *Ghost.*

Going back was not easy. The stormtrooper reinforcements prevented Hera, Sabine, and Zeb from rejoining Ezra and Kanan in the engine room. With the *Sovereign* shaking from internal explosions, the three sprinted to docking bay five, where they crammed into the multicolored TIE Hera called "Sabine's masterpiece."

There wasn't any extra room in the TIE; it was designed to fit one human pilot, and definitely not a Lasat. But Hera didn't want to depart without the rest of her team. "We are not leaving you here on your own!" she commed Ezra. They'd risked everything they had to rescue one of their crewmates, not to lose another.

Kanan's voice came over the comm. "I've got him, Hera. You take care of Zeb and Sabine. Trust me."

Hera was momentarily startled, as she hadn't heard from Kanan for so long. But she was also encouraged. They had made the right choice in disobeying Fulcrum to save Kanan. And the calm confidence in his voice reassured her that he would get both himself and Ezra out alive.

She elbowed Zeb and Sabine aside and launched the TIE out of the docking bay.

In space, she found they were an immediate target for Imperial transports and patrolling TIEs. "We had to take the TIE that had a bull's-eye painted on it," grumbled Zeb.

Hera radioed Chopper for help, but there was no response. She couldn't even see the stolen transport on the scopes.

She banked the TIE to the side, weaving through enemy fire. As good a pilot as she was, she knew that without Chopper's assistance, they were doomed. TIEs had no shields, and one lucky shot could end everything.

"I can't believe that bucket of bolts abandoned us!" Zeb growled.

Hera couldn't, either. But she didn't have time to think about why Chopper would leave them. A TIE came up right on their tail, in range of making a devastating hit, with two more TIEs close behind.

Before their pursuer could fire, a barrage of lasers sent him and the other two TIEs careening away. The Inquisitor's curved-wing TIE took their place.

"We've got your back," Ezra commed.

Hera smiled. Through the canopy she could see Kanan piloting the Inquisitor's TIE fighter. He and Ezra must have taken it from the docking bay. Yet even his help might not be enough. Squadrons of TIEs launched from the other Star Destroyers. The rebels were outnumbered to such a degree that even Chopper wouldn't have been able to calculate the odds of survival if he had been there.

A triumphant melody of beeps chimed over the comm. They sounded like . . . Chopper? Emerging from hyperspace in front of them was none other than the stolen Imperial transport, three blockade runners, and the *Ghost*.

Hera blinked when she saw the diamond-shaped freighter. If Chopper was flying the transport, who was piloting the *Ghost*?

She'd find out soon enough. The blockade runners opened up with their turbolasers, clearing a path for Hera and Kanan to dock their TIEs with the stolen transport. Chopper didn't even wait for them to board to engage the hyperdrive.

Before the starlines appeared, Hera glanced out the TIE's canopy at Mustafar. She could hardly see the planet as the *Sovereign* was ripped apart in a blinding explosion.

CHAPTER 15

Ezra followed Chopper

and the others through the transport's air lock into the *Ghost*. Soldiers in oval helmets stood at attention along the main corridor. Chopper rolled past them, unfazed. At the end of the hallway, the droid projected a holonet feed of a middle-aged man with a mustache.

The man addressed Kanan. "Hello, my friend. It is good to see you again."

Kanan furrowed his brow, where a few more wrinkles had appeared since his capture. "I don't understand. I met you once, for a few moments. I don't even know your name."

"His name is Senator Bail Organa," Hera said.

Ezra started to connect the dots. Not long before, the crew had picked up two droids, C-3PO and R2-D2, who Kanan had returned to the captain of a blockade runner. The man in the hologram must be that captain.

"And the crew of the blockade runner?" Kanan asked.

"Members of other rebel cells," Organa's hologram responded.

Sabine glanced at Hera. "There *are* other cells?"

Since it was all happening so quickly, Ezra found it hard to get a handle on what they were saying. "We're a cell? Did you know we were a cell?" he asked Zeb.

The Lasat appeared as confused as he was. "Um, no."

Hera spoke to all of them. "We weren't supposed to meet. That way, if captured, we

couldn't reveal the other rebels to the Empire. That was the protocol."

A strong, confident voice came from behind them. "The protocol has changed."

Ezra turned to see a rust-skinned woman

climb down from the gunnery ladder. She had head-tails like Hera's, except they were thicker and striped. Ezra had seen others of her species in the city bazaar. They were called Togruta.

"Fulcrum," Hera said.

"Ahsoka. My name is Ahsoka Tano."

"Why did you come here?" Kanan asked.

Ahsoka glanced at Ezra. "Because of you and your apprentice, many in the system and beyond have heard your message. You gave them hope in the darkest times. We didn't want that hope to die."

Chopper wheeled over to Ahsoka. She patted him on the dome. Ezra wondered what their history was—and how Ahsoka had arrived just in time to save them. There were so many questions racing through Ezra's mind. In the end, he decided to ask: "So what happens now?"

Ahsoka looked at him with wide eyes. "I don't know. One chapter is closed for you, Ezra Bridger. This is a new day. A new beginning."

Ezra didn't know this Ahsoka Tano very well yet, but he already liked her, as he liked everyone around him. Hera, Zeb, Sabine, Kanan, and Chopper had plucked him off the streets and given him a purpose beyond pickpocketing. They had taught him that the Empire was not invincible and that he had talents hidden within himself. Time and again, they had risked their lives for him when no one else would have.

Most of all, they had showed him never, ever to lose hope. Hope inspired. Hope was the sun on its rise, bringing the dawn of a new day. And hope could not be defeated.

EPILOGUE

Agent Kallus squinted in the bright sunlight as a shuttle landed at the Imperial complex. The ramp lowered. Grand Moff Tarkin walked out. From what Kallus had learned, Tarkin had escaped in the shuttle before the *Sovereign* blew. The Inquisitor, however, had not been so fortunate.

Kallus stood at attention when Tarkin approached. One would've expected the Grand Moff to be shaken after losing both his flagship and a captive Jedi to the rebels. Yet Tarkin appeared as composed as he had when he first landed on Lothal.

IMPERIAL
STAR DESTROYER

This was a man who refused to admit error, Kallus realized.

"We are getting reports of unrest all over Lothal," Kallus said. "There are whispers from Mustafar. Some people see the Empire as weak, vulnerable."

Tarkin's voice betrayed not a hint of concern. In fact, he smiled. "Not to worry, Agent Kallus. The Emperor has sent me an alternative solution."

The shadow of a figure emerged from the shuttle. First, Kallus heard the heavy breathing, which sounded like the rasp of a powerful engine. Then he saw the swirl of the figure's cloak, a dark shroud that hung from armored shoulders and fell to polished black boots. Last, Kallus's eyes rose to meet the mask. Below two dark lenses, the vented triangle of a respirator replaced a mouth, more menacing than any cruel smile of the Inquisitor's.

Kallus had seen the holonet reports and had heard stories from other officers. But this was the first time he'd seen Lord Darth Vader in the flesh—if there was indeed flesh under all that black armor.

Any doubts Kallus had vanished. The Emperor had committed his greatest weapon to the fight.

The rebels and their fledgling rebellion were doomed.

ABOUT THE AUTHOR

MICHAEL KOGGE has written in the *Star Wars* galaxy for a long, long time. His other recent work includes *Empire of the Wolf,* an epic comic series featuring werewolves in ancient Rome, published by Alterna Comics. He lives online at www.michaelkogge.com, while his real home is located in Los Angeles.